The Boxcar Children® Mysteries

THE BOXCAR CHILDREN

SURPRISE ISLAND

THE YELLOW HOUSE MYSTERY

MYSTERY RANCH

MIKE'S MYSTERY

BLUE BAY MYSTERY

THE WOODSHED MYSTERY

THE LIGHTHOUSE MYSTERY

MOUNTAIN TOP MYSTERY

SCHOOLHOUSE MYSTERY

CABOOSE MYSTERY

HOUSEBOAT MYSTERY

SNOWBOUND MYSTERY

TREE HOUSE MYSTERY

BICYCLE MYSTERY

MYSTERY IN THE SAND

MYSTERY BEHIND THE WALL

BUS STATION MYSTERY

BENNY UNCOVERS A MYSTERY

THE HAUNTED CABIN MYSTERY

THE DESERTED LIBRARY MYSTERY

THE ANIMAL SHELTER MYSTERY

THE OLD MOTEL MYSTERY

THE MYSTERY OF THE HIDDEN
PAINTING

THE AMUSEMENT PARK MYSTERY

THE MYSTERY OF THE
MIXED-UP ZOO

THE CAMP OUT MYSTERY

THE MYSTERY GIRL

THE MYSTERY CRUISE

THE DISAPPEARING FRIEND
MYSTERY

THE MYSTERY OF THE SINGING
GHOST

THE MYSTERY IN THE SNOW

THE PIZZA MYSTERY

THE MYSTERY HORSE

THE MYSTERY AT THE DOG SHOW

THE CASTLE MYSTERY

THE MYSTERY ON THE ICE

THE MYSTERY OF THE
LOST VILLAGE

THE MYSTERY OF THE
PURPLE POOL

THE GHOST SHIP MYSTERY

THE MYSTERY IN WASHINGTON DC

THE CANOE TRIP MYSTERY

THE MYSTERY OF THE
HIDDEN BEACH

THE MYSTERY OF THE MISSING CAT

THE MYSTERY AT SNOWFLAKE INN

THE DINOSAUR MYSTERY

THE MYSTERY ON STAGE

THE MYSTERY OF THE
STOLEN MUSIC

THE CHOCOLATE SUNDAE MYSTERY

THE CHOCOLATE SUNDAE MYSTERY

created by
GERTRUDE CHANDLER WARNER

Illustrated by Charles Tang

ALBERT WHITMAN & Company
Morton Grove, Illinois

Library of Congress Cataloging-in-Publication Data

Warner, Gertrude Chandler, 1890-1979
The chocolate sundae mystery/
created by Gertrude Chandler Warner;
illustrated by Charles Tang.
p. cm. — (The boxcar children mysteries)
Summary: The Boxcar children investigate when
ice cream and other items start disappearing from
their favorite ice cream parlor.
ISBN 0-8075-1146-3 (hardcover).
ISBN 0-8075-1145-5 (paperback).
[1. Ice cream parlors–Fiction. 2. Brothers and
sisters–Fiction. 3. Mystery and detective stories.]
I. Tang, Charles, ill. II. Title. III. Series:
Warner, Gertrude Chandler, 1890-
Boxcar children mysteries.
PZ7.W244 Cj 1995   94-36418
[Fic]–dc20   CIP
                                                 AC

Cover art by David Cunningham.

Contents

CHAPTER   PAGE

1. The Pink Truck   1
2. The Ice Cream Shoppe   10
3. The Angry Customer   22
4. The Disappearing Ice Cream   33
5. Mrs. Saunders   44
6. Benny Has a Dream   57
7. An Evening Walk   71
8. The Trail Is Cold   81
9. A Late Night   95
10. Confession   106
11. A Party   114

CHAPTER 1

The Pink Truck

One spring morning, four children stood outside their house in Greenfield washing the family station wagon. Six-year-old Benny Alden soaked his dirty rag in a pail of sudsy water. "Boy, it's getting hot out here," he remarked to his brother Henry.

Henry, who was fourteen, stood near Benny, carefully polishing the front bumper. "It sure is," he agreed. "When we're done, we could go get some ice cream at the Shoppe."

"Yes!" Benny almost shouted. He grabbed

a clean cloth and vigorously dried the front fenders.

The Shoppe was the oldest ice cream parlor in Greenfield. Benny thought it served the best ice cream in town — even better than the homemade ice cream their housekeeper, Mrs. McGregor, made with her old hand-held crank.

"Ice cream before lunch?" Benny's twelve-year-old sister, Jessie, raised her eyebrows. She tried to sound stern, but secretly she couldn't resist teasing her little brother.

"Please, Jessie, just a small cone," Benny pleaded. He wiped the fender even harder. "I promise it won't ruin my appetite."

"As if anything could," Benny's ten-year-old sister, Violet, said, chuckling. She made sure to wink at Benny so he would know she was teasing. Violet never wanted to hurt anybody's feelings.

"Why don't we just have our whole lunch at the parlor," Jessie suggested. "I think they're still serving tuna and grilled cheese sandwiches." Jessie always had practical suggestions.

"Yes, I'm sure they are," Henry agreed. "I've never known the Shoppe's menu to change."

"Grandfather says the menu is the same as when he was little," Benny pointed out. "They're still using the same ice cream recipes."

"I'll just run in to tell Mrs. McGregor where we're going," Jessie said. Mrs. McGregor, their grandfather's housekeeper, took care of all the Aldens and their dog, Watch. Not that the Alden children needed much looking after. After their parents died, Henry, Jessie, Violet, and Benny had lived all by themselves in an abandoned boxcar in the woods. When their grandfather finally found them, he invited them all to live with him.

The children knew they were really going to love Grandfather when he made sure to give Watch and the boxcar a home, too. Watch lived in the house with the children, and the boxcar was kept in the backyard so the Aldens could visit it whenever they wanted.

Quickly Violet gathered up the dirty rags and put them in a pail of clean soapy water to soak. Henry coiled the hose and hung it on a hook in the garage. Benny put away the car wax and cleaning supplies.

"Mrs. McGregor would like us to pick up a gallon of ice cream for the house," Jessie said as she came running out the front door with Watch at her heels.

"It looks like Watch wants to come with us," Violet said, smiling.

"He can't come into the Shoppe, though," Henry reminded them. "You know they don't allow dogs in restaurants."

"Oh, Watch won't mind waiting outside," Benny said as he clipped a red leash onto Watch's collar. "Almost everyone in Greenfield stops to pet him, don't they, Watch?"

Watch cocked his head at Benny, but suddenly he jumped up and tugged at his leash.

"Hey, do you hear that?" Benny asked.

"Yes, someone is playing some music. It sounds like it's coming from just down the street," Violet said. She ran across the lawn with Benny and Watch at her heels.

"I think it might be an ice cream truck," Jessie said as she and Henry caught up with the others.

Down the street the children could see a bright pink truck with a large green-and-white striped canopy over it. A loud melody sounded from the truck's speakers. White and green balloons were tied to its back fenders.

"I've never seen an ice cream truck like that," Benny said. His big eyes grew even rounder. Already a line of children had begun to form by the truck.

" 'Saunders Ice Cream Treats.' " Violet read the green lettering painted on one side of the truck.

"Look at their flavors — 'hazelnut, lemon-lime swirl, English red raspberry, French vanilla, Jamaican coconut, double fudge chocolate.' " Henry read aloud from the big sign attached to the truck's fender.

"They sound very fancy," Violet whispered as the red-haired girl in front of her ordered a coconut cone with chocolate sprinkles. The Aldens stood off to one side so the woman selling the ice cream would not think they were in line.

When the last customer had been served, the tall blonde woman behind the counter leaned out the truck's window. "Are you in line? May I help you?" she asked. She even leaned further out the window of the truck so she could see the children better. The woman wore a bright red and gold sweater. Her thick blonde hair was pulled back with a large glittery gold bow. The deep, red nail polish on her fingers matched her lipstick.

"Uh, no, we were just looking," Jessie answered politely. "Are you Mrs. Saunders?"

"Yes," the woman answered proudly. "I own this business and the truck."

"Maybe we should bring Grandfather and Mrs. McGregor back a carton of one of these fancy flavors," Violet suggested to Henry under her breath.

"I bet Grandfather would like some hazelnut ice cream," Henry answered just as softly.

"What's that? Speak up," the woman called.

"Oh, Violet, I really wanted to get our ice cream at the Shoppe," Benny said more loudly than he meant to.

At the mention of the Ice Cream Shoppe, the woman's face fell. "Well," she said huffily, "if you just want plain old-fashioned ice cream with no flavor."

"The Shoppe's ice cream has flavor," Benny couldn't help saying.

The woman rolled her eyes. "I can tell you children don't know much about ice cream."

Watch picked that moment to start barking at a squirrel. He pulled at his leash, as the squirrel raced up the tree.

"Please get that dog away from my truck," the woman said, noticing Watch for the first time. "It's not sanitary for animals to be near food."

"We were just leaving," Henry answered. His sisters had already turned to go. Benny gave Watch's leash a firm tug.

"You know," the woman called after them. "The Shoppe never tries new flavors, and what's more, they've never remodeled their store. Their kitchen is probably filthy."

Benny stared at the woman. He was so angry, he could feel his face turning bright red. "That's not true!" he cried. "The Shoppe makes the best ice cream in Greenfield."

"And their kitchen couldn't be cleaner. We've seen it," Jessie called as she put her arm around her little brother. "Come on Benny. Let's just go to the Shoppe."

CHAPTER 2

The Ice Cream Shoppe

"I wonder what that lady has against the ice cream parlor?" Jessie asked thoughtfully when the Aldens were further down the street.

"Maybe she's just mad the Shoppe is taking customers away from her business," Henry suggested.

"She had lots of customers," Benny pointed out as he stopped to wait for a red light.

"She did. But she probably knows it's going to be hard to keep up with a place as popular as the Shoppe," Violet said as the Aldens crossed the street.

"She didn't have to be so rude." Benny still felt upset. Without saying anything more, he helped Violet tie Watch's leash to a tree.

"I know what you mean," Jessie said sympathetically. She nodded at Benny before opening the door to the Ice Cream Shoppe.

"Hey, wait, Jessie, did you see this sign?" Henry said, as he pointed to the parlor's big window. Violet read the sign aloud:

HELP WANTED
APPLY WITHIN

"That's strange," Jessie said thoughtfully. "The Shoppe doesn't get much turnover. People hardly ever quit."

"I hope Tom still works here," Benny remarked as the children went inside. Tom had worked in the parlor for as long as Benny could remember. Benny liked Tom because he always gave Benny an extra big scoop of ice cream and remembered to put

extra cherries on the children's sundaes.

The Ice Cream Shoppe had a black and white tiled floor. Bright red and white lamps hung from the high ceilings. There were red leather booths facing the large picture windows and high stools by the wooden counter. In the middle of the parlor were small tables with marble tops, and chairs with comfortable red cushions.

Behind the counter hung a large mirror in a wooden frame. As long as the children could remember, an old-fashioned clock had ticked loudly in front of the mirror. Today the children noticed the clock had stopped.

"Oh no, I hope nothing's wrong with that big clock," Benny whispered sadly.

"Well, it was old; it probably got tired of running," Jessie said. She tried to sound comforting, but Benny looked even sadder. He didn't like it when anything in the parlor changed.

Quickly he stole a look behind the counter. He was relieved to see the shiny row of glass containers holding peanuts, cherries, chocolate sprinkles, and other sundae toppings, just the way he remembered.

"Let's get a booth," Henry suggested as his sisters grabbed some menus from the counter.

"Oh, look, they have fresh strawberry ice cream," Violet said as she settled herself in the soft leather booth. She scooted over to the window to make room for Jessie.

"Do you think Tom is working here today?" Benny asked as he looked around the large sunny room.

"I don't see him," Henry remarked. "You know, this place seems different."

"You mean because of the clock," Benny suggested as he pored over the colored drawings of sundaes, banana splits, and other goodies on the menu.

"Not only because of the clock, Benny," Henry said.

"Well, there aren't many customers here today," Violet observed.

Henry nodded his head. "That's just what I was thinking."

At lunchtime, the parlor was usually so

crowded it was hard to find a seat. Today nearly every booth was empty and only two people sat at the big counter.

"Maybe that ice cream truck is hurting the parlor's business after all," Henry said grimly.

"I just can't believe it could," Violet shook her head. "We should ask Ruth about this." Ruth was the waitress who usually worked the lunchtime shift.

"I don't see her working, either," Jessie said as she took some napkins out of the dispenser and passed them around to her family.

"No," Henry shook his head. "In fact, I don't recognize the waitress on duty at all."

Jessie and Violet turned to look at the dark-haired girl behind the counter. She had short black hair, almond-shaped eyes, and very fair skin. She wore a red-and-blue T-shirt underneath her white apron.

The girl caught Violet's eye. "Someone will be right with you," she told the Aldens as she continued to mix a chocolate ice cream soda for one of the customers at the counter.

The children noticed she spoke with an accent.

"I wonder where she's from," Benny whispered.

"Hard to tell," Henry answered. "You know," he continued, "it's strange there's no one here we know."

"Yes," Jessie agreed. "Where are Mr. Richards and Pete?"

Mr. Richards, the elderly owner of the parlor, usually came around to all the booths to visit with the customers. His grandson, Pete, worked in the Shoppe as a cook.

"Excuse me, I couldn't help overhearing your conversation." A short, round man came toward their table. He wore a sparkling white apron over his rather large stomach. "I'm afraid Mr. Richards and Pete no longer work here."

"But Mr. Richards is the owner," Jessie sounded so surprised she raised her voice.

"Not anymore, I'm afraid. He sold the parlor to me last week," the man answered. He smiled at the Aldens, but he could see how sorry they were to hear his news.

"Why did he do that?" Benny couldn't stop himself from asking.

"The Shoppe was getting to be too much for him," the new owner explained.

"It's true, he was very old," Jessie said.

"Do Tom and Ruth still work here?" Violet asked. "We know them very well." Though Violet was sorry to hear about the changes at the Shoppe, she found she liked the new owner's open, friendly face. In fact, she thought he looked a little bit like Santa Claus with his twinkly blue eyes, bushy white beard, and red cheeks.

The man stopped smiling and shook his head. "No, Tom and Ruth left last week," he answered abruptly. "They both got jobs that paid more. I'm hiring a whole new staff."

"We saw your sign in the window," Benny said sadly. He forgot, for an instant, how hungry he had been. "Does that mean everything will be changing?" He was afraid to hear the answer.

"No, not at all. The parlor's always been so popular. Why fix what isn't broken?" The owner looked so cheerful again, the children didn't want to ask why business seemed so slow.

"Oh, I'm glad to hear that!" Benny sounded very relieved. "I think I'll order a chocolate sundae."

"Good for you," the owner said, chuckling. He turned around and called to a young boy carrying a tray of banana splits. "Oh, Brian, come wait on this table next, please."

Brian couldn't have been more than twelve years old. He had fine blond hair and lots of freckles. He was tall and thin. "I'll be right there," the boy answered, nodding to the owner.

"I'm hoping working here will fatten him up a bit," the owner confided to the Aldens. "Well, I have to get back to the kitchen. I hope to see you all again."

"Oh, you will," Jessie assured him. "This is our favorite place to eat in Greenfield."

"Good," the owner said. Before he left their booth, he introduced himself as Mr. Brown.

"He really should be Mr. Red because of

his red cheeks," Benny blurted out when the owner had gone back into the kitchen.

"Ssh, Benny, he might hear you," Jessie said, giggling into her napkin.

"I think Benny's right," Henry said, winking at his brother. They went back to their menus and didn't even notice Brian standing by their booth.

"Excuse me. Are you ready to order?" the waiter asked softly.

The Aldens didn't seem to hear him. Brian gulped and looked down at the floor before asking again, this time more loudly.

Henry looked up a little sheepishly. "I'm still trying to decide." He sounded apologetic.

Jessie and Violet ordered tuna salad with lettuce and tomato, and dishes of strawberry ice cream for dessert.

"The strawberry ice cream was just made today," the boy said, looking at Violet. He seemed glad to have something to say to her.

"Are you new here?" Violet asked.

Brian blushed. "Uh, I started last week," he muttered while he looked down at his notepad and busily wrote their orders.

"Do you like working here?" Benny asked after he'd ordered his grilled cheese sandwich and a chocolate sundae with extra chocolate sprinkles on the side.

"Oh, yes, I really like the ice cream," Brian said, smiling.

"Me, too," Benny said.

Brian grinned so widely his eyes crinkled. "Your sandwiches will be out in a few minutes," he said.

As Brian hurried away, Benny noticed a group of four boys hovering outside, near the front door. The boys were dressed in old T-shirts and pants that looked too big for them.

The tallest of the group tried to get Brian's attention by knocking on the window. When Brian looked in the boys' direction, the tall boy held up his hand and quickly opened and closed it.

"Why don't those boys just come in?" Benny wondered aloud.

"What boys?" Jessie asked, raising her eyebrows. Her back was to the window.

Quickly Benny explained what he had seen. By the time Jessie and Violet turned around to look, the boys were gone.

"Excuse me! This still isn't a good ice cream soda. You put too much fizzy water in it! Can't you understand simple directions?" The loud voice of an angry customer interrupted the children's conversation.

"Who's he talking to like that?" Violet asked, rather shocked.

"To that new waitress up at the counter," Henry answered pointing with his head. The Aldens turned.

The customer waved his hands in the air as he tried to tell the waitress how to make his soda. By mistake, his hands hit his glass. His soda spilled all over the counter.

A young woman sitting a few seats away jumped up to avoid staining her white linen skirt. The waitress looked as if she were about to cry.

CHAPTER 3

The Angry Customer

"Hey, what's going on out here?" Mr. Brown called as he came hurrying out of the kitchen. "That's no way to talk to one of my waitresses," he told the man angrily. "She's new here, new to this country, and she's never worked in an ice cream parlor before."

"That's obvious," the man answered. He was very tall, and when he stood up, he towered over Mr. Brown. Without saying another word, he stormed out of the parlor. He didn't even stop to pay for his lunch.

"Well, good riddance to him," Mr. Brown said, shaking his head at the waitress. She managed a small smile then buried her head in her hands.

"Why don't we help clean up the counter?" Jessie suggested. "They seem very short of help."

"Good idea," Henry said. Hastily, the Aldens gathered up some napkins. Henry and Violet began mopping the counter. Jessie cleared away a soggy sandwich.

Mr. Brown wiped his hands on his big apron. He patted the new waitress gently on the arm. "Simone, please don't cry," he said gently. "I've just been so busy this week, I haven't had time to train you properly. It's not your fault we lost that customer."

Benny quietly handed Simone some napkins so she could dry her eyes. "Thank you," Simone said, smiling at Benny.

"Where are you from, Simone?" Jessie asked gently.

"I'm from France," Simone answered proudly. "I came here for the summer to improve my English."

"Your English is excellent," Violet said with admiration.

"I studied it a long time in school," replied Simone modestly.

Mr. Brown looked thoughtfully at the Aldens. Benny was now wiping the far end of the counter. Henry had gathered all the soggy napkins and was throwing them away in the trash.

"I can see you children are hard workers," Mr. Brown said. He looked very impressed. "Would you be able to help Simone and Brian this afternoon — after you've had your lunch? We don't have a big staff yet, as you can see."

Before the children could answer, Brian hurried by carrying a tray of sandwiches. "Oh, Mr. Brown, one of your suppliers is at the back door. What should I tell him?" the young waiter called.

Mr. Brown sighed. "I'll be right there."

"I think those sandwiches are for us." Benny eyed the tray hungrily.

"Please children, sit down and have your lunch. Then, if you'd like, we'll put you to work this afternoon. By the way, can you make sodas and milkshakes?"

"I think we could," Jessie answered. "We always used to watch Tom and Ruth work behind the counter."

"Oh, would you show me?" Simone begged. She dabbed her eyes with a napkin.

"Sure," Jessie said with a grin.

Mr. Brown sighed with relief. "That would be wonderful," he said. "Until we hire a cook, I don't have much time to be at the counter. I'm so busy making ice cream and sandwiches." Mr. Brown paused as if noticing other customers at the counter for the first time. "I'll get you another sandwich," he told the young woman in the white skirt.

"Thank you," she replied, smiling at Mr. Brown. "I think that man was very rude."

"He's been in here before," Simone said, shaking her head. "He's always complaining about something."

"Really?" Mr. Brown frowned.

"Yes," Simone continued. "Yesterday, he said his vanilla milkshake wasn't mixed correctly, but he drank it anyway. He said he knew how to make much better ones."

Mr. Brown sighed and shook his head.

"I told him I was sorry he didn't like his shake," the waitress continued. "He said he couldn't understand how I could be working here when I didn't know how to do anything."

"So today when he came in, he gave you instructions?" Mr. Brown said kindly.

"Yes, but you heard what he said about his ice cream soda." Simone looked sad.

"I heard him," Mr. Brown answered grimly. "Did he at least pay yesterday?"

"Yes, but he almost threw the money on the counter," Simone replied.

"If he comes back, let me know," Mr. Brown said abruptly. "I'd like to talk to him. Now you must excuse me. I have to get back to the kitchen. I'll be right out with your sandwich," he told the woman in the white skirt.

While the Aldens ate their lunch, they could not stop talking about the strange customer.

"It sounds like that man just wanted to make a big scene," Henry remarked as he stirred his vanilla milkshake.

"I wonder if there really was anything wrong with his soda," Jessie said thoughtfully. She bit into her sandwich.

Henry sipped his milkshake. "This one tastes just fine," he said.

"Yes, but Mr. Brown probably made that milkshake. It came from the kitchen, not the counter," Violet reminded him.

"That's true," Henry said. He took another long sip.

"Why do you think that customer came back," Violet asked, "when he didn't like what he had yesterday?"

"Maybe he is going to tell everyone about the problems here," Henry said. He wiped his hands on his paper napkin.

"Hey, maybe he works for Mrs. Saunders," Benny suggested. He sat up a little straighter.

"We'll just have to keep our eyes on him," Henry said. He added some salt to his sandwich. "I wonder if he'll come back."

Benny nodded. He licked the last bit of chocolate sauce from his long spoon. "This ice cream sundae is as good as always," he said happily.

After lunch, the children cleared their table themselves because Brian was very busy. "At least they're getting more customers," Violet remarked to Jessie as several mothers with young children came in.

Jessie and Violet went behind the counter to help Simone. Benny grabbed a broom and swept the floor, and Henry worked in the kitchen making sandwiches.

The next customer at the counter ordered a strawberry ice cream soda. Jessie called Simone over so she could watch Jessie make it.

Carefully, Jessie measured the strawberry syrup and milk. She poured the ingredients into a tall glass and stirred them. Then she added soda water.

"See, I'm leaving some room at the top of the glass for the ice cream," Jessie said as she dropped a big scoop of strawberry ice cream into the glass. She then added a little more soda water and some whipped cream.

"Oh, you make it look so easy," Simone said. She made a vanilla soda while Jessie looked on. The customer said it was delicious.

"Oh, I've learned so much," Simone told Mr. Brown at the end of the afternoon. "I can now make milkshakes, sodas, and malteds."

"I'm glad, Simone," Mr. Brown said encouragingly. "I knew all along you could, but I'm glad you feel more confident." He turned to the Aldens.

"I can't thank you enough," he told them. "With Henry making all the sandwiches, I had time to make enough ice cream to keep up with our orders for the week."

"That's good. We need more chocolate and vanilla ice cream at the counter," Simone mentioned.

"All right, I have some in the kitchen freezer," Mr. Brown said. "I'll fill those containers before I leave this evening."

"Could you teach us how to make ice cream sometime?" Henry asked.

"Of course, my boy. I'd love to." Mr. Brown seemed delighted. "Just as long as you don't peek when I put in the secret ingredients that make the parlor's ice cream so special."

The Aldens nodded.

"Good," Mr. Brown said approvingly. "You see, I promised Mr. Richards I would never give away his secrets." Mr. Brown paused. "You children wouldn't be willing to come help us for the next couple of weeks?" he asked hopefully. "You've been such a big help to us already."

The Aldens all looked at one another. They were all thinking the same thing. "We'd love to," Jessie finally answered for them.

Mr. Brown grinned. "Good, come by in the morning. We open around nine o'clock." The Aldens nodded.

"And before you go, let me give you some ice cream to take home to your family — on the house," Mr. Brown said. He pressed a gallon of freshly made peach ice cream into Henry's arms.

"What does 'on the house' mean?" Benny whispered to Violet.

"It means we don't have to pay for it," Violet explained. "He's giving it to us as a present."

Benny smiled. "I like presents like that."

"Good," Mr. Brown said as he opened the door for the children. "See you tomorrow."

Watch was waiting patiently outside, in the shade.

"Oh, Watch, I hope you weren't too lonely," Benny said as he untied the dog's leash from the tree.

"I visited him when things got a little slow in the kitchen," Henry said. "Lots of people stopped to pet him. He seemed to be all right."

On the way home, Benny skipped down the sidewalk. "I can't think of a better place to work than the Ice Cream Shoppe," he said happily. "Wait until we tell Grandfather!"

CHAPTER 4

The Disappearing Ice Cream

That evening, the children's cousins Joe and Alice came for dinner. They brought their seven-year-old daughter, Soo Lee, with them. Joe and Alice had adopted Soo Lee from Korea.

"I can't believe you'll be working in the Ice Cream Shoppe," Alice said as she passed the salad to Jessie. The Aldens were all seated at the long dining table. "We'll make sure to visit you there, won't we, Soo Lee?"

Soo Lee swallowed a bite of her meatloaf and nodded. "I like ice cream," she answered, looking a bit sadly at the pile of green beans on her plate.

"I hope you come when I'm working behind the counter, Soo Lee," Benny told his cousin. "I'll put lots of sprinkles on your ice cream." Benny knew Soo Lee liked chocolate sprinkles almost as much as he did.

Soo Lee smiled and took a bite of her green beans. She was pleased to find they didn't taste too bad.

"There's just one thing that worries me a little," Grandfather said as he poured himself some lemonade from the big red pitcher.

"What's that, Grandfather?" Henry held his fork in midair.

"Well," Grandfather said as he handed the lemonade pitcher to Violet, "don't you think it's strange all the old help quit at once?"

"Well, yes," Henry admitted. "I'm hoping we can find out why when we're working there."

Grandfather's blue eyes twinkled. "I'm sure you will," he said. Grandfather was very proud of the way his grandchildren had solved so many mysteries in the past. They had helped many people. Maybe now they could help the Ice Cream Shoppe.

The following morning, Henry, Jessie, Violet, and Benny were up early. They ate breakfast with their grandfather at the round table in the kitchen.

"We'll expect you back for dinner with an appetite," Mrs. McGregor teased the Alden children as they hurried out the front door.

"Oh, we'll be working too hard to eat much ice cream," Benny assured her. The others laughed.

The Aldens decided to ride their bicycles to the Shoppe.

"Spring is my favorite time of year," Violet said to Jessie as they pedaled along the flower-lined streets. Violet's bicycle was purple, her favorite color. It matched the lilac trees that were now in full bloom.

When the Aldens arrived at the Shoppe, they entered through the kitchen. "Boy, am I happy to see you," Mr. Brown greeted them.

Henry grabbed an apron from the big hook

in the kitchen. The others did the same.

"Brian couldn't come in today, and we've already had some customers. They've been buying out my fresh peach ice cream." Mr. Brown sounded tired.

"How did people know about it?" Benny asked.

"Oh, I made a sign for it this morning," Mr. Brown explained. He sighed and mopped his brow with a clean white handkerchief. "You know, I don't think I've stopped working since I bought the parlor."

"I could make signs for you," Violet volunteered.

"No one draws better than Violet." Benny sounded proud.

"Oh, could you?" Mr. Brown looked at Violet with relief. "Here, you can do today's menus. That would save me some time. I keep some colored pencils over there." Mr. Brown pointed to a large drawer under the kitchen counter.

"Where's Simone?" Jessie asked.

"Oh, she'll be a little late this morning. She had some errands to do."

Jessie looked at Henry, but she didn't say anything. She thought Mr. Brown had a lot to do all by himself.

Violet set right to work at a little table in the corner of the kitchen. Jessie served ice cream at the counter, and Benny helped Henry prepare the sandwiches.

Simone finally came in just before lunch. She was wearing a pink T-shirt that said *I am not a litterbug.*

"That's a nice shirt," Jessie remarked.

"Thank you," Simone said, turning so Jessie could see the design on the back — a cartoon of a dog carrying his bone to the garbage can.

"I just love American T-shirts," Simone said as she reluctantly tied on her apron. "I just bought three new ones this morning." She pointed to her big shopping bag.

Jessie wondered why Simone had spent the morning shopping when Mr. Brown seemed so busy. But she didn't have time to think about Simone for very long.

It was lunchtime and the parlor was busier. For the next hour, Jessie, Benny, and

Simone took turns waiting on tables or serving people at the counter. Jessie and Simone prepared most of the counter orders.

The first few customers ordered chocolate floats. Jessie scooped out the ice cream with the parlor's pink scooper. She saw there wasn't much chocolate ice cream left in the container.

"Oh, Benny, would you please run to the kitchen and get some more chocolate ice cream? We're running out." Jessie scooped out all the chocolate ice cream she could, then handed Benny the metal container.

Benny opened the swinging door to the kitchen. Violet sat at the table mixing a big bowl of tuna salad. Mr. Brown was heating some cream on the stove.

Benny tried with all his might to open the freezer door.

"Oh, let me help you with that, Benny," Mr. Brown said as he took his big pot off the stove.

"I didn't know you had to cook ice cream." Benny sounded puzzled.

Mr. Brown chuckled and moved his chef's

hat further up on his head. "You don't. You just have to heat the cream, sugar, and vanilla together before you put it in the ice cream maker," he explained as he tugged open the freezer door. "Now, what did you need in here, Benny?"

"More chocolate ice cream." Benny held out the metal container.

Mr. Brown seemed puzzled. "I just refilled that container last night. I thought there was enough to last a week," he said as he grabbed another big carton from the freezer. But when he looked inside, he saw it was empty!

Mr. Brown looked at Benny with raised eyebrows. He rummaged through the other cartons in the freezer, but he couldn't find any more chocolate ice cream.

"I don't know what happened to it," he told Benny. "Maybe business has been better than I thought."

Benny and Mr. Brown came back to the counter empty-handed. "Jessie, I can make more chocolate ice cream, but it won't be ready for a couple of hours," Mr. Brown said.

"Oh, dear," Simone groaned. "Everyone is asking for chocolate today, and the lunch rush is just beginning."

"We'll just have to talk people into ordering the fresh peach ice cream. There's lots of that," Benny said. He hurried away to wait on two teenagers with blond ponytails.

Mr. Brown shook his head. "I know I filled that container of chocolate ice cream last night. Did you get a lot of customers earlier this morning?"

"No," Jessie answered. "I didn't even notice it was low until I got my first order." She wiped some marshmallow sauce off the counter. "Oh, by the way, do we have more chocolate sauce?"

"Are we out of that, too?" Mr. Brown sounded surprised. He pushed on the spigot from the large jar holding the sauce. "You're right, we are low," he said shaking his head. "I'll have to make more. Once the rush is over, could one of you please help me in the kitchen?"

Jessie nodded. "I'd love to," she volunteered. Jessie had always wanted to see how the Shoppe made its creamy chocolate sauce.

"This is a mystery," Simone told Jessie when Mr. Brown had left. Her blue eyes twinkled. "We can call it, 'The Mystery of the Missing Ice Cream.' "

Even though she was worried, Jessie giggled. But she wondered why Simone didn't seem more upset.

Simone topped a strawberry sundae with some cherries. "Well, at least we're not out of cherries," she remarked.

"Or peach ice cream," Jessie added as she turned on the blender to mix a peach milkshake.

"Jessie, what's a parfait?" Benny asked loudly above the whir of the blender.

"It's layers of ice cream and different toppings in a tall glass," Jessie answered. "Why?"

"Well, those girls want to split a strawberry parfait." Benny nodded toward the two girls with ponytails.

"Okay, I'll get a tall glass. I saw some here yesterday," Jessie said as she looked under the counter. The pretty tall glasses were missing!

"Maybe they're in the kitchen being washed," she told Benny. "Let's check."

Benny and Jessie looked and looked. So did Violet and Mr. Brown, but no one could find the tall parfait glasses. "Let's wait and look some more after the rush is over," Mr. Brown suggested.

"I can't understand it," Jessie told them. "I saw six of those glasses under the counter yesterday afternoon."

Mr. Brown shrugged his shoulders. "We have more," he said. "I'm just not sure where they are."

"What should I tell those girls?" Benny asked.

"Why don't you offer to give them a strawberry sundae on the house," Mr. Brown suggested.

"Okay," Benny said. Mr. Brown really likes giving things away on the house, Benny thought to himself. He even *acts* just like Santa Claus.

CHAPTER 5

Mrs. Saunders

Simone and Jessie tried their best to convince their customers to have the fresh peach or strawberry ice cream.

"When you have your heart set on chocolate, it's hard to change your mind," a young woman grumbled.

"I know what you mean," echoed a police officer. He looked at the menu again but couldn't find anything else he wanted. "I just don't like ice cream with fruit in it," he said handing the menu back to Jessie.

"What about vanilla?" Jessie suggested.

"No, thanks. I think I'll just go to the donut shop."

"I'd have vanilla," said a woman in a straw hat. "But you don't even have any chocolate sauce to put on it, isn't that right?"

Jessie was forced to agree.

"What's happened to this place since Mr. Richards retired?" the woman in the hat shook her head. "Let's go, Delores," she said to her companion. "Maybe we can find that new ice cream truck. They must have chocolate."

Simone looked at Jessie and rolled her eyes.

Jessie felt very sorry for Mr. Brown. She knew that if he was at the counter, he'd be offering to give everyone free ice cream.

After the rush, Jessie went to the kitchen to help Mr. Brown make more sauces. She left Simone deep in conversation with a red-haired young man. Jessie wondered why they were whispering.

"Oh, there you are," the owner said when

he saw Jessie. "I have a fresh batch of chocolate in the ice cream maker."

Jessie nodded. She didn't have the heart to tell Mr. Brown about all the customers they'd lost at lunchtime.

For the next hour Jessie and Violet measured out chocolate, butter, sugar, milk, and vanilla extract for the sauce. Then they heated the mixture over the stove, stirring it constantly with a big wooden spoon.

"Oh, this smells wonderful," Violet said as she stirred the large saucepan.

"It makes me want to lick the spoon," Jessie answered.

"I'm glad I'm not the one making it," Benny observed. "Or I would only be licking the spoon and not cooking." His sisters laughed.

Jessie and Violet made four batches. They did let Benny taste it. "That should be enough to last us for awhile," Violet said as the sauce cooled on the counter.

"Tomorrow, we'll make butterscotch and raspberry sauce," Mr. Brown said. "I don't want to run out of anything again."

Jessie and Violet nodded.

Mr. Brown looked at his watch. "Well, it's going to be time to close in about an hour," he said. "You must be tired."

"I feel fine," Violet said. "Me, too," Jessie said as she washed out the mixing bowls and put them in the dishwasher.

"Don't rinse the big wooden spoon!" Benny almost yelped. "Can't we lick it?"

"Sure, Benny," Jessie said, handing it to him.

Violet wiped her hands. "I think I'll help Simone at the counter. She must need a break."

"Well, I don't know," said Jessie. "She's still talking to that red-haired guy."

The only customers Violet found were a mother and her little girl. They were sharing a butterscotch sundae. The girl was upset her white poodle had to be left outside.

"I could go play with him," Simone offered. "Violet can take my place at the counter." Violet nodded.

"Oh, would you just see how she is?" the

little girl asked. She looked at Simone with big blue eyes.

"Oh, really, Angela," the girl's mother said. "There's no need to bother the waitress. Pebbles will be fine. We're not going to be here very long."

"Oh, I don't mind. I would like the fresh air," Simone assured the mother.

Violet had not been at the counter long when she heard a familiar voice.

"That poodle outside your store almost bit me!" a woman said as she came into the parlor and collapsed in a booth. Violet knew the woman right away. She was Mrs. Saunders, the owner of the pink ice cream truck.

"Pebbles wouldn't bite anyone," cried the little girl at the counter.

"Goodness!" said the girl's mother. "Are you all right?"

Mrs. Saunders nodded and said "I think so," in a low quavery voice. Then she took a small pocket mirror from her purse and carefully examined her reflection. She powdered her nose and reached up to straighten the pink bow in her hair.

"At least, I *think* I'm all right," she continued in the same tone of voice. "I've just had a bad shock. You see, I don't like dogs," she admitted. "And they don't like me."

"What happened exactly?" the mother asked.

"I was just walking down the street," Mrs. Saunders began in a much stronger voice, "when that dog began to bark at me. It barked very loudly I must say."

"Pebbles doesn't have a loud bark," Angela protested.

"*Ssh* Angela," her mother warned. "Please don't interrupt." Angela scowled at Mrs. Saunders and blew bubbles in her milk with a straw.

"Luckily, a girl was holding that animal," Mrs. Saunders continued more loudly now that she had everyone's attention. "Or I'm sure he would have bitten me."

"Pebbles is a girl dog," Angela commented.

"Angela, quiet," her mother said wearily. "I'm sorry this happened," she said, turning to Mrs. Saunders. "We're glad you're not hurt." Angela frowned, but she didn't say anything more.

"May I get you anything, Mrs. Saunders?" Violet asked, coming over to her booth with a menu.

Mrs. Saunders looked curiously at Violet. "Oh, do you know my ice cream truck? Is that how you know my name?" She sounded pleased.

"Well, yes," Violet admitted.

"You could bring me a glass of water." She looked at Violet more closely. "Aren't you one of the children who wouldn't buy my ice cream? You had a dog with you."

Violet nodded. She felt her cheeks flush.

"Well," Mrs. Saunders said fanning her face with her menu. "I didn't know you worked in the parlor."

"Would you like to try any of our ice cream?" Violet asked politely.

"Yes, I could try it." Mrs. Saunders sounded like she was doing Violet a favor. "What about a small sample of your fresh peach? I hear from my customers you're out of chocolate." Mrs. Saunders looked smug.

Violet nodded.

"Do you have samples? I just want to taste it. I don't want to pay for a whole portion," Mrs. Saunders said.

"Well, I'll have to ask the owner," Violet answered.

Simone came back in the parlor just as Violet was bringing Mrs. Saunders her glass of water. The waitress carried a piece of paper with some writing on it. When she saw Violet looking at her, she hurriedly folded the note and put it in the pocket of her apron.

Twenty minutes later, Mrs. Saunders had enjoyed a glass of lemonade on the house. She had also sampled the strawberry, vanilla, and peach ice cream. In exchange, Mrs. Saunders had agreed to bring Mr. Brown small samples of her ice cream to taste the following day.

"It's too bad the chocolate isn't ready," Mrs. Saunders said as she wiped her mouth with her napkin. "But may I try your hot fudge sauce?" She leaned back in the booth.

"Mrs. Saunders, we're getting ready to close up now," Mr. Brown said gently. "I can give you some hot fudge to take with you."

"Oh, thank you. And maybe some strawberry and butterscotch sauce, too. Just enough to taste now," she called after Mr. Brown.

Henry exchanged glances with Jessie. "Mrs. Saunders, what made you change your mind about the Shoppe's ice cream?"

"Well, I'd never tried it before. It's old-fashioned, but it isn't bad. Not bad at all."

"Isn't there anything you would like to *buy* here, Mrs. Saunders?" Henry hinted. "What about a small cone?"

Mrs. Saunders frowned and looked at her watch. She checked it against the big clock at the counter. "Your clock has stopped," she said.

"Yes, we know," Mr. Brown called as he came out of the kitchen. He placed three small paper cups, all wrapped, in front of Mrs. Saunders. "It's very old. I'm trying to find someone who can fix it."

"Well, I must be going," Mrs. Saunders said. Reluctantly, she rose out of the booth and carefully put the samples in her large bag. On the way out, she did buy a small — very small — vanilla cone.

"I know Mrs. Saunders was trying to be nice, but I still don't trust her," Henry said as the children pedaled home through the park.

"Me neither." Benny was out of breath. He had to pedal very hard to catch up with Henry.

"I know what you mean," Violet said. She was just behind Benny. "Mrs. Saunders looked very pleased we'd run out of chocolate ice cream this afternoon."

"That probably improved her afternoon business," Jessie remarked.

"I wonder if Mrs. Saunders took that chocolate ice cream," Henry said. He pedaled more slowly so Benny could keep up with him.

"And the missing glasses and hot fudge sauce," Benny reminded them.

"There could be another reason all those things are missing," Violet said.

"Like what?" Benny turned around to look at Violet with raised eyebrows. His bicycle swerved a little on the dirt road.

"Maybe Simone or Brian broke those glasses, and didn't want to admit it," Violet suggested.

"It's true," Henry agreed. "It would be easier for one of them to be responsible for the missing things since they both work there."

Then Violet told the others about Simone not wanting her to see the note she carried.

"But," Jessie protested, "why would Simone or Brian want to take anything from Mr. Brown? He's so patient and kind — always giving food away. Even if Simone or Brian broke those glasses or ate up the chocolate ice cream, Mr. Brown probably wouldn't take any money out of their salaries or fire them."

The others were forced to agree. "We'll just have to keep our eye on all of them — Mrs. Saunders, Simone, and Brian," said Henry.

"What about that angry customer we saw the first day?" Violet asked.

"He's suspicious, too," Jessie said, nodding. She playfully rang her bicycle bell so Benny would let her pass in front of him. "I'll race you home," she called to Violet and her brothers.

CHAPTER 6

Benny Has a Dream

That night, Benny had a dream. He was working in the Ice Cream Shoppe surrounded by cartons and cartons of all different kinds of ice cream — banana, chocolate, raspberry, vanilla, blueberry, and peach.

In his dream, Benny wore a big white chef's hat. He spooned the creamy chocolate ice cream from its container and put it in a tall glass. Suddenly more and more glasses appeared. Feverishly, Benny tried to put a scoop of ice cream in each one, but he couldn't keep up. The glasses clicked against one another. Some of them broke and shattered all over the Shoppe. . . .

Suddenly Benny woke up. Somthing was rattling outside his window. He sat straight up in his bed. Was this part of his dream?

Sleepily, Benny tumbled out of bed and peered out the open window. It was very windy and a tree branch lashed against the house. "That's probably what I heard," Benny muttered under his breath.

As he drifted off to sleep, he thought he heard boys' voices in the distance.

The following day, Benny woke up when Henry playfully tossed a pillow at him.

"Benny, better get up. Don't you want to come to the Shoppe with us?" Benny opened his eyes and saw Henry, Jessie, and Violet crowded around his door.

"Hello, sleepyhead," Jessie teased. "Do you know what time it is? Almost nine o'clock."

Benny turned on his side. "You know, I dreamed about the Shoppe last night."

He moved his stuffed bear, Stockings, out of the way so his sisters and brother could sit on the bed. "I dreamed I was the chef."

"Did you wear a big hat?" Violet liked knowing what everybody wore.

"Yes," Benny murmured. "I was surrounded by all different kinds of ice cream. And some glasses broke. Then I heard a noise outside my window and woke up."

"Well, Sir Chef," Jessie said, getting up to give Benny a bow. "You should invent a new ice cream dish at the Shoppe and name it after yourself. That's what chefs do."

Benny laughed. "Maybe I will," he said.

A half hour later, Henry, Jessie, Violet, and Benny were heading quickly down the sidewalk to the Shoppe. As they stopped at the corner to wait for a car to pass, Jessie looked down and stepped out of the way of some broken glass.

"Watch out!" she warned the others.

Benny looked down next to his red sneakers. "Broken glass," he said. "You know I dreamed about broken glass."

"Yes, you told us," Violet said thought-

fully. "You dreamed some glasses in the parlor broke." She stepped carefully so the glass wouldn't cut her new lavender sandals.

"You mean the parfait glasses we couldn't find yesterday?" Jessie suddenly looked very interested. She bent down to examine the glass more carefully. So did Violet.

Just beneath the curb Jessie found a big piece that looked like it could be the rim of one of the missing parfait glasses. Jessie held it up and looked very excited.

"We shouldn't jump to any conclusions," Henry cautioned. "Somebody may just have dropped their groceries. For all we know, this could be a jar of peanut butter."

"If that's true, how come there's no peanut butter or food around?" Benny wanted to know.

"Good point," Jessie said. "Benny did you hear anything else last night?"

Benny looked thoughtful. "I remember waking up for a minute. I think I heard some boys talking but it seemed far away. Then I went right back to sleep."

"Did they sound like young boys or teenagers?" Violet wanted to know.

Benny scratched his head and shrugged his shoulders. "They were just boys," he said. "Maybe about Henry's age."

Before they left, the Aldens picked up more pieces of glass and carefully put them in Jessie's handkerchief.

"There," Jessie said as she tied the handkerchief. "If we do find more parfait glasses in the Shoppe, we can see if the glass looks the same."

When they arrived at the Shoppe, the Aldens found Brian and Simone hard at work. Brian was helping Mr. Brown make sandwiches in the kitchen. Violet noticed that Brian had dark circles under his eyes, and his clothes were rumpled.

Simone stirred some butterscotch sauce on the stove. She was wearing yet another new American T-shirt. This one had a pink background and pictures of different colored ice cream cones printed on it.

"I wish I had a shirt like that," Benny said with approval. "I could think about ice cream all day long." Everyone laughed, except

Brian. He mixed mayonnaise into a large bowl of tuna and yawned.

"Brian, you're looking very tired. Am I overworking you?" Mr. Brown asked. He said it teasingly, but he looked worried.

Brian shook his head. "No, I was just up a little late last night," he said as he squeezed some lemon juice over the tuna salad.

Mr. Brown nodded. "Well, see how you're feeling, my boy. Maybe you can leave early."

Brian shook his head. "No thanks," he muttered. "I'll be all right."

At lunchtime, Jessie, Brian, and Benny worked behind the counter while Violet and Simone waited on tables. Henry made sandwiches in the kitchen.

"Mr. Brown, did you ever find those missing glasses?" Henry asked. He added pickles and potato chips to a plate holding a grilled cheese and tomato sandwich.

Mr. Brown shook his head. He stirred more sugar into the pot of caramel sauce he was cooking. "No, I never did, but I've been too busy to look more carefully," he said.

At the counter, Benny topped a strawberry sundae with whipped cream and a cherry. "Thanks, Benny," Jessie said as she took the sundae from her brother and placed it in front of a man in a pin-striped suit.

The man took a spoonful and made a face. "Oh, waitress," he said. "Your whipped cream is sour!" The man pushed the sundae away from him.

"I'm very sorry. I'll make you another one with fresh cream from the kitchen."

"No, thank you," the man answered. He shook his head. "I'm not hungry anymore."

Several other customers at the counter looked at Jessie and Benny in disgust. A woman in a blue smock dress eyed her chocolate milkshake suspiciously. "I don't think I want to taste this," she said. "There's whipped cream on it."

Jessie nodded and took the drink from the woman. "Can I make you another one?"

"No, thank you. I'll just finish my sandwich."

By then, the customers sitting in the booths had also complained. Simone, Brian,

Violet, Jessie, and Benny collected many ice cream dishes from unhappy customers. Only two people decided to reorder.

When Benny went to get more whipped cream from the kitchen, he found the other jars had spoiled as well.

"I don't understand it," Mr. Brown said. He frowned. "Those jars were all in the refrigerator."

"Did the power go off last night?" Henry asked.

"I don't think so." Mr. Brown rummaged through the refrigerator. "If it had gone out, these cartons of ice cream would have melted. Everything is frozen solid," he reported.

Henry frowned. "Someone must have left the cream out for a long time."

Mr. Brown nodded. "That's true," he said. "That's how it could have spoiled. Oh, Simone," he called to the waitress as she came in to pick up her order.

"Yes," Simone looked up. She held two plates of tuna sandwiches.

"Did you refrigerate the cream at the

counter yesterday?" Mr. Brown asked.

"Of course." Simone sounded surprised by the question. "I always do."

"I know you do," Mr. Brown said reassuringly. He looked at Henry and shrugged. "We kept all the other jars refrigerated the whole time we worked here yesterday."

Henry nodded. "Did we have the refrigerator open a long time?" he asked.

"No, I don't think so. But I'll ask your sisters. They were in here helping me make the chocolate sauce."

Jessie and Violet did not remember leaving the refrigerator open. Violet looked very upset. "I hope we didn't leave the door open by mistake," she told Mr. Brown.

"It's possible we could have left it open when we took out the ingredients we needed, and thought it was closed," Jessie said. She looked unhappy too.

"You have to slam it shut, don't you?" Violet asked.

"Don't worry, girls. I don't think you left it open," Mr. Brown said kindly. "I check it every so often. Now you'd better get back to your customers."

Jessie sighed. "We're not really that busy. A lot of customers left because they were upset about the cream."

Mr. Brown shook his head. "Well, at least they seem to be eating lots of sandwiches." Mr. Brown tried to sound cheerful, but Jessie and Violet could tell he was worried.

"I don't like this," Mr. Brown continued. "If we have more days like this, the Shoppe will lose its good reputation, and I'll have to close it up."

"Is something wrong?" Brian said as he came in the kitchen to refill the salt and pepper shakers. He noticed how sad everyone looked, especially Violet.

"We were just wondering how all the cream spoiled," Mr. Brown told him.

"Oh," Brian said. He unscrewed the tops of the salt shakers and concentrated on pouring more salt into them.

"Well, Brian, at least I don't have to ask you any questions," Mr. Brown said as he patted Brian on the back. "You weren't even here yesterday." Violet thought Brian looked a little uncomfortable.

"Soo Lee! Alice! You came!" Benny called out a few minutes later. He motioned his cousins toward the counter. Soo Lee returned Benny's smile and climbed up on a stool.

"Well, hello Benny, where are all your customers?" Alice asked as she put her soft leather purse down on the counter. Alice remembered better days when there was a line out the door for the Shoppe's ice cream.

"We had some trouble with our whipped cream today," Benny explained. "It spoiled."

"Oh, I'm sorry to hear that," Alice said.

"So were we," said a man at the counter who was reading a newspaper. "I was really looking forward to an old-fashioned hot fudge sundae."

"Couldn't you have it without the whipped cream?" Alice suggested.

The man sipped his lemonade and turned a page of his newspaper. "No, it wouldn't taste the same," he said without looking up.

Alice raised her eyebrows. "What do you recommend for Soo Lee and me?" she asked Benny.

Before Benny could answer, Jessie and Violet came out of the kitchen. Benny thought they seemed upset, but their frowns faded as soon as they saw Alice and Soo Lee.

"Oh, you came to visit!" Jessie exclaimed as she hugged her cousins in turn.

"Are you hungry?" Violet asked them.

"I was just asking Benny's advice about what we should order," Alice answered.

"You know," Benny said very seriously. "I'd like to make you a sundae I invented. I've been thinking about it all day."

"Oh, Benny, you are becoming a real chef!" Jessie exclaimed. "May we watch?"

"Sure," Benny said as he wiped his hands on his apron. "The best thing about this sundae is you don't even need whipped cream."

The man at the counter stopped reading his paper and looked up. Carefully, Benny spread fresh ripe cherries in the bottom of a sundae dish. He put a generous scoop of vanilla and chocolate ice cream on top. Then he added thick dark chocolate sauce on the vanilla, and marshmallow topping on the chocolate ice cream.

"Could you hand me the jar of chocolate sprinkles please?" Benny asked Jessie.

He sprinkled on nuts and chocolate sprinkles, placed two cherries on each mound of ice cream, and handed the dish to Alice and Soo Lee.

"Oh, Benny, that looks wonderful," Alice exclaimed. Soo Lee had already picked up her spoon.

"It does look good," the man with the newspaper admitted grudgingly. "May I have one, too?"

"Benny, you saved some of our lunch business with that sundae," Mr. Brown said proudly at the end of the day. "I'm going to name it after you and have Violet list it on the menus. We'll call it the Benny Special."

Benny flushed with pleasure.

CHAPTER 7

An Evening Walk

As the Aldens walked home, they saw Mrs. Saunders' ice cream truck parked two blocks away from their house. Six children were in line for ice cream.

"Yoooo-hoooo," Mrs. Saunders called when she saw the Aldens. "How was business today?" She handed a raspberry cone to a girl with brown pigtails.

"Not very good, I'm afraid," Henry was forced to admit.

"Oh, I'm sorry to hear that," Mrs. Saunders said as she took the girl's change. The

Aldens didn't think she looked sorry at all.

"You really should make sure your cream stays fresh." Mrs. Saunders said as she adjusted her flowered headband.

The Aldens looked at one another. "How did you know our cream was spoiled?" Benny couldn't help asking.

"Oh, some of my customers complained about it," Mrs. Saunders answered. "Wouldn't you like to try some of *my* ice cream today? It's very fresh."

"No, thanks, we're not hungry," Benny answered for all of them.

"I can't believe how rude she is," Jessie said angrily when the Aldens were inside their house. She was so upset she didn't even stop to pet Watch as he came bounding over to greet her.

"Jessie, what's the matter?" Grandfather called. He sat in the living room reading the newspaper in his big overstuffed armchair.

Grandfather listened closely while his grandchildren told him all that had happened in the parlor, including their meeting with

Mrs. Saunders. "Grandfather, don't you think Mrs. Saunders must have something to do with all that trouble in the parlor?" Jessie asked.

Grandfather shook his head. "I don't know what to think." Grandfather folded his paper and put it on the table beside him. "But I do know you all have been working very hard. Why don't we take Watch for a walk in the park and forget all about the parlor this evening."

"That sounds good to me," Benny said happily.

"We'd better leave now so as not to be late for dinner," Grandfather said as he put on a jacket.

As the Aldens walked to the park, they were happy to see that Mrs. Saunders' truck had pulled away from their street.

"I'm glad we don't have to talk to her anymore today," Benny remarked.

When they arrived in the park, Benny unclipped Watch's leash. Watch took off at once to chase after some squirrels. An Irish setter followed him.

"Hey, Watch! Watch! Come back!" Benny called.

Grandfather chuckled. "Oh, let him get his exercise. He's been in the house all day," he said.

"Look, all the cherry trees are in bloom," Violet exclaimed.

"The park does look pretty," Grandfather said looking at the rows of tulips along the park's edge. The branches of the cherry trees stirred in the wind. Some petals dropped on the ground as the Aldens walked across a great lawn.

"Oh, I see Watch!" Jessie exclaimed. "He's down by the pond."

"Why don't we find a stick for him?" Benny suggested. Henry followed Benny into the woods behind the pond. They had not gone very far when they heard a loud voice behind some trees.

Henry put his fingers to his lips. He was sure he'd heard that voice before. It was the voice of the angry customer who had yelled at Simone the first day.

The man was talking loudly again. "I know

I could do a better job than that girl," he was saying to someone. "I've been trained as a waiter. It wasn't my fault the old man fired me so fast! I'll show them!"

Benny looked at Henry with big round eyes. He didn't say a word.

"Take it easy, Joe," the man's companion was saying. "You can't be so mad all the time and expect places to jump at the chance to hire you."

"But I know I'm better than most people who have those jobs!" Joe exclaimed. "I'm a professional waiter!"

Just then Benny stepped on a twig.

"What was that?" Joe cried. Benny took a few steps backward and looked helplessly at Henry. Henry shook his head as if to tell Benny not to worry. The boys were hidden from the men by thick oak trees.

"Don't be so jumpy, Joe! It's probably just someone walking by. This is a public park, you know."

"You don't have to be such a wise guy, Larry," Joe said irritably. "I know it's a public park." The men's voices faded away as they continued on their walk.

Benny and Henry waited until the men were safely out of sight before they left the woods.

"Didn't you find a stick for Watch?" Jessie asked her brothers when she saw them come toward her empty-handed.

"Oh, Jessie, you'll never guess what we heard!" Benny exclaimed.

"We saw that angry customer in the woods," Henry said.

"Now boys, catch your breath and tell us exactly what happened," Mr. Alden said. Jessie nodded and motioned everyone over to a park bench. Watch, who by that time had grown tired of chasing squirrels, came with them. He lay down by Jessie's feet.

Quickly Henry told his family the whole conversation between Joe and his friend. "But that doesn't prove Joe is responsible for all the trouble in the parlor," Henry added.

"No, it doesn't," Jessie was forced to agree. "Do you think the Shoppe fired him?"

"If they did, it must have been Mr. Richards who let him go," Violet suggested. "Be-

cause Mr. Brown didn't even seem to know him."

"That's true, and we've never seen him either," Henry said as he rolled down the sleeves of his sweater. "It's getting colder out here," he remarked.

"Yes, the sun is going down," Grandfather said. "We should start home."

"Besides," Jessie reminded them all as they got up to leave, "how would he get in to take all the ice cream and those glasses?"

"You know, I don't think Joe is to blame," Henry said. "But if the parlor did fire him, that could explain why he's so rude whenever he comes in."

When the Aldens crossed Greenfield's Main Street, they noticed the street cleaners were out. The cleaners carried big hoses and were washing the sidewalk. Watch tried to lick the pavement.

"You're thirsty, aren't you Watch," Grandfather remarked. "We'll be home very soon," he assured the dog.

"The parlor looks quiet tonight. No lights are on, and everything is locked up," Henry observed as they walked by.

"Mr. Brown must have finally gone home," Violet said as the Aldens crossed the street.

On the way up their driveway, the Aldens decided Mrs. Saunders was still the prime suspect. "But how does she get into the parlor to take all the ice cream and glasses?" Violet asked. She unzipped her lavender windbreaker as Grandfather opened the front door.

"That's what we have to find out," Henry said as he stepped inside and unclipped Watch's leash.

"I hope Simone and Brian aren't helping her," Jessie said. She hung up her navy blue jacket in the hall closet.

"I just can't believe they would be." Violet sounded sad.

Henry sighed. "We have to suspect everyone in the parlor, I'm afraid," he said as he went to wash his hands before dinner.

Before they went to bed that evening, the Aldens met in Benny's room to think of a plan. They decided Jessie and Violet would report to work at the parlor the next morning. Henry and Benny would ask for the day off to trail Mrs. Saunders' pink ice cream truck on their bicycles.

"Does that mean we have to eat her ice cream?" Benny asked as he leaned back against his red pillows.

"Well, no," Henry said thoughtfully. "I don't think we should draw attention to ourselves. We should just spend a day watching her to see what she does."

"Are you going to tell Mr. Brown why you want the day off?" Violet wondered.

The others shook their heads. "No, I think for now it's best not to worry him," Henry decided.

CHAPTER 8

The Trail Is Cold

The Aldens left for work early
the next morning with Watch. "Henry and
I can take him for a walk after we talk to Mr.
Brown," Benny explained.

"But won't he keep you from your detective work?" Jessie asked. "You know how
Mrs. Saunders dislikes dogs."

"Oh, we'll drop him off at home when we
come to pick up our bicycles," Henry said.
Watch wagged his tail and nuzzled Henry's
knee. He loved it when the Aldens took him
for a morning walk.

As soon as the Aldens were down the street from the Shoppe, they knew something was wrong. Mr. Brown and two police officers were roping off the entrance to the Shoppe.

"What happened?" Benny cried as he ran toward the entrance. The others soon caught up with him. At once they could see the parlor's big picture window had been smashed. Pieces of glass lay all over the sidewalk.

"Watch your step. Don't cut yourself on the glass," one of the police officers warned them. "And keep that dog away from here," the other one said.

Mr. Brown greeted the Aldens with a grim face. "Good morning," he said. "As you can see, we've had some excitement here."

"When did this happen?" Henry asked.

"I don't know," Mr. Brown answered shaking his head. "I found it like this when I arrived early this morning. I think I'm going to have to close the parlor today. I put Brian and Simone to work in the kitchen making ice cream."

"Oh, could Violet and I stay to help them?" Jessie suggested politely.

"Well, if you insist, I won't say no," Mr. Brown answered. He looked at Jessie kindly, but Jessie could tell his mind was still on the broken window. As if reading the children's thoughts, Mr. Brown added, "But I won't be needing all of you. We won't have any customers today."

Henry looked at Benny. "That's fine Mr. Brown," Henry said. "Benny and I can just take the day off."

Mr. Brown nodded absentmindedly. "Very well, I'll see you boys tomorrow then."

Henry turned to Watch. "And now you can get your morning walk, Watch. Would you like that?"

Watch was not paying any attention. He strained at his leash and sniffed the ground, trying to go closer to the broken window.

"Watch, what's the matter?" Henry asked.

"There's some strawberry ice cream that dripped onto the street. It's by the broken glass. He probably wants to lick it," one of the police officers suggested. Henry looked down and saw that a trail of strawberry ice cream led down the street.

"Do you know how the window got broken?" Henry asked the officer.

"That's the strange thing," Mr. Brown answered for everyone. "The police seem to think it was broken from the inside because the glass is all *outside*, on the sidewalk. But I can't believe it. I left the parlor securely locked last night and there's no sign of a break-in."

"Was anything taken from the parlor?" Henry asked. "Like more ice cream?"

"No, not that I noticed," Mr. Brown answered, but he sounded a little unsure. The Aldens looked at one another.

"I'll check the container of strawberry ice cream," Jessie muttered to Henry as she waved good-bye to her brothers and Watch.

"Do you know how far this trail of strawberry ice cream goes?" Benny asked the police.

"Oh, that," one of the officers answered. "There's bound to be ice cream dripped on the ground near an ice cream parlor," she said. "I wouldn't pay too much attention to it."

Benny looked at Henry. "Why don't we follow it," he suggested. Henry shrugged and nodded. He had to tug Watch's leash very hard before the dog finally budged.

When Watch saw there was more ice cream down the street, he wagged his tail and finally started walking. "Don't lick it, Watch!" Henry protested as Watch sat down at the street corner where there seemed to be a lot of ice cream.

"Whoever it was must have stopped to wait for a red light," Benny suggested. Henry nodded.

The boys followed Watch and the ice cream trail all the way down the next block. There was much less ice cream on the street now, and Watch soon lost interest.

"You know, Benny, we may very well be on a wild goose chase," Henry told his brother. "Lots of people walk down these streets with their cones or cartons of ice cream dripping. Anyone could have spilled part of their cone, just like the police said."

Watch had now stopped to look at a cat. The cat climbed further up into the branches of one of the oak trees that lined Greenfield's Main Street.

"I know." Benny sounded a little disappointed. "But don't you think it's strange that only strawberry ice cream is on the sidewalk this morning? And it looks pretty fresh," he added.

"That's true," Henry said thoughtfully. "We did sell lots of other flavors yesterday." Henry paused to tell Watch to stop barking at the cat. Suddenly, his eyes lit up.

"Benny, don't you remember they were cleaning the streets last night!" Henry exclaimed.

Benny nodded excitedly. "Yes! That proves this ice cream was spilled *after* the Shoppe closed. And it leads right from the broken glass. I'm sure this is a good clue." Benny couldn't wait to ask Jessie if she'd noticed any missing strawberry ice cream.

"We might as well keep following this trail and see where it goes," Henry suggested.

The boys continued down the street with
Watch. The trail of ice cream led them toward an alleyway.

Benny looked closely at the ground. He
could see a spot or two of pink ice
cream.

The boys followed the trail through the
alley and down a side street. When they
thought they had reached a dead end, Henry
found smudged pink fingerprints on the
fender of a car and on a store window. So,
off they went again. The trail skirted the side
streets and led down another alley.

"I'm really glad this person was a slow
eater," Benny said as he hurried to keep up
with Henry and Watch.

"A slow and messy eater," Henry said,
"judging from all the fingerprints we've seen
so far." Soon the boys were in a very run-
down section of Greenfield.

"This is where the old textile mill used to
be," Henry said. Henry and Benny could
see old abandoned buildings in the distance.
Garbage littered the sidewalk. They walked
by small houses with broken windows and

overgrown yards, where junked cars had been left to rust outside.

"You know, I think we've come to the end of the trail," Henry said. The boys stood in the front yard of a small house that was badly in need of repair. The porch steps sagged. The paint was peeling, and the yard was overgrown with weeds and dandelions.

Just then a woman came out of one of the houses down the street. "Are you boys looking for someone?" she asked.

"Uh, we were just walking our dog," Benny explained.

Henry cleared his throat. "You know, we were looking for some ice cream," he said.

"Ice cream?" The woman gave Henry a blank look.

"Yes, ice cream," Henry repeated. "You don't know of anyone around here who brought home a lot of strawberry ice cream last night, do you?"

The woman smiled. "Sorry," she answered shaking her head. "I know lots of people who would like ice cream, but the children around here can't afford to buy much."

Henry and Benny nodded.

"Well, you'd best be going on home now," the woman advised. "Do you know where you're going?"

"Yes," Henry said tugging at Watch's leash. The boys turned around and walked up the street. They didn't look back. If they had, they would have seen the woman staring after them. When Henry and Benny turned the corner, she walked up to one of the houses and knocked on the door.

Jessie and Violet spent their morning in the Shoppe's kitchen. As soon as she could, Jessie checked the supply of strawberry ice cream at the counter. She opened the glass case, which always had steam on it because the ice cream was so cold.

She picked up the container of strawberry ice cream and looked at it closely. It didn't have a small layer of frost on it like the others did. She was almost sure the container looked emptier than it had yesterday.

"Well, at least no one cleaned us out," she thought to herself. But it looked as if someone had taken enough to make a few cones. Jessie decided she would count the number of cones and cartons in the supply closet before she left.

Jessie and Simone spent the day preparing salads for the next day's lunch. Jessie washed lettuce and cut up tomatoes. Simone made a big bowl of chicken salad.

Around noon, Mr. Brown told Simone she had a visitor. Simone went out to speak to him and left Jessie cutting up celery.

Jessie quickly excused herself and went outside. Without being too obvious, Jessie followed Simone and her friend down the street. When they stopped at the corner, Jessie popped into the drugstore across the street so she could still watch them.

"May I help you?" the woman at the counter asked Jessie. Jessie bought a small package of tissues and continued to look out the window.

Simone and her friend talked without ever looking up. Jessie looked at Simone's companion more closely. She knew she had seen him before. He was the red-haired customer who often talked to Simone at the counter.

Simone and her friend kept talking. The sales clerk in the drugstore gave Jessie a strange look. Jessie wished there was some way she could hear what Simone was saying.

After a few minutes, though it seemed much longer to Jessie, Simone waved good-bye and started walking back to the Shoppe. She never noticed Jessie following her across the street.

Meanwhile, Violet helped Brian and Mr. Brown make more ice cream toppings. Brian worked very hard all day. He didn't talk much. And Violet didn't see him doing anything at all suspicious.

Henry and Benny decided to have a snack when they got home with Watch. As they ate the peanut butter sandwiches Mrs. McGregor prepared, they told her all about their morning.

"Do I have to eat that?" Benny asked pointing to the plate of salad Mrs. McGregor had placed in front of him.

"Yes," Mrs. McGregor said smiling. "It will give you energy while you bicycle after that ice cream truck."

"We better leave soon," Henry said as he looked at his watch. "I think she starts making her rounds before noon so she can get the lunch crowd."

Benny swallowed some salad. "I'm ready," he said.

Henry and Benny found Mrs. Saunders' truck parked near the Ice Cream Shoppe. There was a long line of customers. Henry and Benny hid themselves and their bikes behind some bushes across the street near the drugstore.

When at last Mrs. Saunders' truck moved on, the boys were ready. They followed her all over Greenfield. Everywhere they went, it was the same. Mrs. Saunders received customers, handed out cones or ice cream bars, and took her customers' change.

"This is boring," Benny said as he put his bicycle on the ground and crouched behind yet another tree trunk.

"I'll say," Henry agreed. "She's so busy she's not talking to her customers."

It was almost dark when Mrs. Saunders began to count up all her money. She closed the windows of the truck and took her menu down. The boys followed her as she parked the truck in a lot near the school, then walked to a house nearby. They watched her go in her front door and turn on the light.

"I'm afraid we're not going to have too much to tell Jessie and Violet about Mrs. Saunders," Henry said as the boys pedaled home. Benny nodded wearily.

"But you know, Mrs. Saunders locks up her truck almost the same time as the Shoppe closes," Henry observed. He looked at Benny. Benny looked too tired to talk.

"So," Henry continued as he turned his bicycle at the corner, "she *could* be the one who breaks into the parlor late at night."

"Maybe, but right now I'm too tired to think about it," Benny moaned.

"But not too tired to eat dinner, I hope," Henry teased.

Benny laughed and shook his head.

CHAPTER 9

A Late Night

That night at dinner, Jessie lost no time telling her family about the missing strawberry ice cream.

"Why didn't Mr. Brown notice it was missing?" Benny wondered aloud.

"There was still lots of ice cream in the container, just not as much as yesterday," Jessie replied as she passed the meatloaf to Henry.

"Whoever is taking ice cream is being more careful now," Violet observed as she poured herself some water. "They're making sure to leave some so we won't notice it's missing."

"You should all be very proud of your-selves. You put in a good day of detective work," Grandfather said. He gazed affec-tionately at the tired faces of his grandchil-dren. Benny looked so sleepy, he could barely hold his fork up to eat the delicious meatloaf Mrs. McGregor had made.

"Oh, I forgot to tell you the good news," Violet said as she poured some milk into Ben-ny's cracked pink cup. That cup was very special to Benny. He'd had it ever since they'd lived in the boxcar.

"What?" everyone but Jessie said at once.

"Mr. Brown had a new glass pane installed this afternoon. The Shoppe can now open for business tomorrow."

"Oh, that is good news," Grandfather re-marked as he put some pepper on his mashed potatoes.

Jessie proceeded to tell her family about Simone and her mysterious friend. Everyone listened closely.

"That's not the same customer who yelled

at her the first day?" Benny wanted to make sure.

"No," Jessie replied. "This is another one. He has red hair — and he's very quiet. I've seen him with Simone before."

"Maybe they are planning something," Henry said thoughtfully as he poured himself some water. "But I still can't believe Simone is really involved in all this. She seems so careful about her work."

"Well, she did take the morning off after all that chocolate ice cream disappeared. And one day Violet saw her reading a note very secretively," Jessie reminded Henry. "I don't want to believe it of Simone either," she added.

Henry and Benny took turns telling their family about the ice cream trail they'd followed.

"You know," Jessie said, "I wonder if there's a connection between the ice cream trail and that trail of broken glass we saw."

"You mean the morning after I heard glass breaking," Benny said after he swallowed a mouthful of peas. He tried not to make a face.

"Yes!" Jessie sounded excited.

"There may be," Henry said. "I just don't know what to make of all these clues yet."

After dinner, the children gathered in Benny's room again to come up with another plan.

"I think we're going to have to keep an eye on the parlor one evening after Mr. Brown closes up," Henry said.

Jessie nodded. "There's a big closet in the kitchen we can hide in."

"Oh, the one where Mr. Brown keeps the brooms and mops," Violet said. "It would be big enough for all of us to fit in."

"Good," Henry said. "We should wait a couple of nights, I think."

"Why?" Benny asked and then yawned.

"I think whoever broke that window will probably stay out of sight for a couple of days," Henry remarked.

The others nodded. Then they all went to bed early and slept soundly.

* * *

The Shoppe was quiet for the next two days. Business seemed very slow. The Aldens watched Simone and Brian closely, but they never saw them do anything out of the ordinary.

The following Monday, the Aldens came to work early. Mr. Brown was already in the kitchen mixing a big batch of creamy chocolate ice cream. "I'm putting chocolate sprinkles and cherries in this batch," he announced. Benny grinned.

Violet went to the table to get today's menus, and right away she noticed something was wrong. Someone had scribbled on the menus with green crayons.

Mr. Brown looked at the menus in disbelief. "Simone, Brian, do you know anything about this?" he said calling the others to the kitchen.

Simone and Brian shook their heads. "I can make more menus," Violet said. She tried to put Mr. Brown at ease.

"I know you can," the owner answered sadly. "But that's not the point." He sighed.

"I didn't believe this at first, but someone is really trying to hurt the parlor," he said, looking at everyone gathered around him.

"Surely, you don't think we're responsible." Simone sounded a little indignant.

Mr. Brown sighed even more heavily. He sat down at his stool by the ice cream maker. "No, I would hate to think anyone in this room is responsible," he said. "But I lock up at night. And most mornings when I come in something has been disturbed."

Simone looked down at the floor.

"At first, I thought I was just forgetting or misplacing things," Mr. Brown continued. "I am absentminded, but now I'm convinced someone wants to hurt our business."

The Aldens looked at one another. "But who would want to hurt the parlor's business?" Simone asked. She looked down at her hands and twisted her silver ring around her index finger.

"Have you thought about Mrs. Saunders?" Benny asked.

"Or what about that customer who is always so angry?" Simone asked Mr. Brown.

"That's possible," Mr. Brown said. The Aldens noticed how sad and tired he looked. "If any of you see anything suspicious, I hope you will let me know."

"Of course," Simone said. The others nodded and went back to work.

That afternoon, when no one else was around, the Aldens secretly made plans to spy on the parlor late that evening.

"We'll have to be careful," Jessie whispered as she added maple syrup to a banana shake. "Now that Mr. Brown is so suspicious, he'll be very careful about locking up. He may even look in the closet."

"I didn't think of that," Henry said. "Maybe we should tell him what we're planning."

Violet shook her head. She drew some soda water from the spigot at the counter. "I don't think he'd let us do this, if he knew."

"You're probably right," Henry said. "The fewer people who know of our plan, the better."

* * *

That night Mr. Brown said he felt very tired. He began to lock up the Shoppe around five o'clock in the afternoon. The Aldens waited until Brian and Simone had left. Then, while Mr. Brown was in the kitchen putting on his coat, they pretended to leave by the front door.

"Good-bye, Mr. Brown," they called.

"Good-bye, children. See you tomorrow," Mr. Brown said.

Henry pretended to close the door with a loud bang. Then quickly, the Aldens all sneaked into the small coat closet at the far end of the counter.

Luckily for them, Mr. Brown only came into the parlor's main area to lock the front door. Then he returned to the kitchen and left by the back door, locking it firmly behind him.

"Whew, it feels good to get out of there," Benny said as he emerged from the cramped closet.

"I know what you mean," Henry said. He stretched his arms out in front of him and rubbed his shoulders. "It was crowded inside

with all of us. It's a good thing the broom closet in the kitchen has more room."

"I'm just glad we didn't disturb anything," Jessie said as she let Violet crawl out in front of her. Violet was careful not to pull down any of the aprons that hung crisply on their hangers.

"I'm afraid we may have a long wait ahead of us," Henry whispered. "I'm going to call Grandfather from the pay phone to tell him where we are, and that we'll be home by nine o'clock."

"Be careful not to let anyone see you from the window," Jessie warned him.

"Don't worry, the shades are down," Henry whispered back.

"Why are we all whispering?" Benny wondered. "We're the only ones here."

For the next three hours, the Aldens played word games and ate the sandwiches Henry had saved from lunch. At about eight o'clock, the parlor was dark.

"It's spooky in here when the sun goes down," Benny said softly.

"We should have brought a flashlight," Henry observed.

"I know where we can find one," Jessie said. No sooner had she pulled a flashlight from a big drawer, than they heard someone rattling the back door.

"Someone's trying to get in!" Benny whispered loudly.

"Quick!" Henry said. "Into the storage closet." The Aldens hurried inside amongst the mops and brooms as the rattling grew louder and louder. Benny's heart was pounding so loudly he was sure everyone could hear it. But he kept still. Finally, when he thought he couldn't stand the suspense any longer, the back door creaked open.

Someone turned on the kitchen light and a muffled voice said, "Okay, come in."

CHAPTER 10

Confession

Benny gulped. Henry peered through the keyhole. What he saw made him shake his head sadly.

Brian was leading four skinny boys into the parlor's kitchen. The boys wore T-shirts that looked much too big for them, and worn-out shoes.

As Henry watched, Brian seated the boys at the big kitchen table. "Can we have chocolate sundaes tonight?" one of the boys asked.

"Sure," Brian said. "You know this is the

last night we can do this," he added as he went to the counter to bring back the container of vanilla ice cream.

"But Brian, you promised," the tallest boy protested.

"I know, Eric," Brian said as he scooped out four generous portions of vanilla ice cream and put them in special sundae dishes. "But the owner knows something is up."

"Was he mad about those glasses we broke?" one of the boys asked.

"No," Brian said as he poured chocolate sauce on the ice cream.

"We didn't do it on purpose," Eric said. He got up to help Brian finish making the sundaes. "Paul tripped on a crack in the sidewalk and dropped the package."

"I don't think Mr. Brown even noticed those glasses," Brian said as he put cherries on all the sundaes. "But we have to remember to put everything back in the refrigerator. One night we left the cream out and it spoiled."

"I guess it didn't help when we broke that big window," Eric said glumly. "But we were just trying to help you clean up. I was chasing Paul with the broom and the next thing I knew, the handle went through the window."

"I know you didn't do it on purpose," Brian said as he brought the sundaes to the kitchen table with Eric's help. "But we should have tried to keep Robbie from scribbling on the menus."

The boy called Robbie shook his head sadly. "I'm sorry, Brian," he said softly.

Brian patted the little boy's shoulder. "I know you were very excited when you saw all those crayons in the kitchen drawer."

Brian seated himself at the table while the boys ate hungrily. Henry, who was still watching through the crack, noticed that Brian did not eat anything himself.

"Oh, I'm starving," the boy called Paul said as he scraped the bottom of his dish. "This is the first meal I've had all day."

For some time now, Benny's foot had been asleep. He shifted uncomfortably and tried to wiggle his foot. It tingled so much, he jumped and banged against Jessie, who gave him a warning look in the dark. Benny moved the other way and knocked over the big mop. It clattered loudly to the floor and hit Violet.

"Ouch!" she yelped, then quickly clapped her hands to her mouth.

The boys in the kitchen all jumped and looked toward the closet.

"What was that?" Eric said. He stopped eating and held his spoon in midair.

"Something fell down in the closet," Brian answered.

"I heard someone talking in there," Eric insisted. He advanced warily toward the closet, still holding his spoon.

Henry took that moment to open the closet door and step out. Jessie, Violet, and Benny followed him.

The boys stared at the Aldens in horror. "Who are you?" Eric asked sharply.

"It's okay. I know them. They work here," Brian explained.

He turned to the Aldens. "I know what you must be thinking," he said sheepishly. "I can explain."

"Maybe we should leave now," Eric said quietly. Brian nodded.

When the boys had left, Brian sat at the kitchen table and told the Aldens everything, everything they hadn't already guessed.

The boys lived at the edge of town in a very run-down neighborhood. Brian was very good friends with the oldest one.

"Is that Eric?" Benny asked.

"Yes," Brian nodded. "When he heard I had a job here, he thought I'd be able to help him and his little brothers. You see, Eric's father lost his job a year ago and his family is very poor. Sometimes, this is the only meal they get all day."

At first the Aldens had been angry at the boys for eating the Shoppe's ice cream without paying. Now they felt so sorry for them they nodded sympathetically.

"Could Eric get a job at the parlor?" Jessie suggested. "I'm sure Mr. Brown would hire him."

Brian shook his head. "No, he has to stay home and baby-sit his little brothers. His mother works, and his father left the family a few months ago."

Jessie looked down at her hands. "I see," she said gently.

Brian shifted uncomfortably in his chair. "I knew what I was doing was wrong," he said. "But they'd all come to depend on me."

"How did you get in?" Henry wondered.

Brian's face turned bright red. "We used a coat hanger to pick the lock," he admitted. "We never broke it."

"I know," Henry said. "That's why Mr. Brown never found any sign of a break-in."

Brian pulled a notebook out of his apron. He lay it on the table and opened it to a page filled with a neat row of numbers. "I was keeping track of what they ate and how much it cost," he explained. "I was planning to pay Mr. Brown back out of my salary. But after that window broke, I didn't know what to do."

Henry patted Brian gently on the arm. "Don't worry, Brian, we believe you," he said. "But you have to tell Mr. Brown about all this."

Brian hung his head. "I know I do," he said. "I feel awful that I helped ruin the parlor's good reputation."

"It's not ruined yet," Jessie assured him. "Once all this is explained, the customers will be back in no time."

Brian smiled, giving Violet a shy admiring look.

The following day, the Aldens and Grandfather came to the Shoppe a little late. They wanted to give Mr. Brown and Brian plenty of time to talk.

When they arrived, Mr. Brown had his arm around Brian. "I can't thank you enough for getting to the bottom of this mystery," Mr. Brown said when he saw the Aldens.

The Aldens beamed and proudly introduced Mr. Brown to their grandfather.

"If I'd known your grandchildren were going to stay here after closing, I wouldn't have allowed it," Mr. Brown said shaking his head. "But I'm glad they did," he added, winking.

"I just told Mr. Brown the whole story,"

Brian said, "I have to work at the parlor one month for free." He looked at Mr. Brown and grinned. "But Eric and his brothers can still come to the Shoppe and get a free treat every week."

Grandfather said, "I'll talk to Eric's parents. I'm sure the children and I can help in some way."

"Yes," Mr. Brown said nodding. "I'll also give them our leftover food. We always have lunch fixings left over at the end of the day. That would be better for them than ice cream."

"All I have to do now is think of a way to bring customers back to the parlor," Brian said.

"You know," Jessie said grinning, "I think I have an idea."

CHAPTER 11

A Party

A week later, Grandfather drove his whole family over to the Shoppe in the big station wagon. Soo Lee, Joe, and Alice came too.

A big sign that said OPEN HOUSE hung over the Shoppe's front door. Inside, white and red balloons hung from the Shoppe's ceiling. Streamers draped the counter. A big long table at one end of the parlor held several cartons of fresh, homemade ice cream in silver buckets of ice.

"Yum, there are fresh berries and cherries

cut up into some of the ice cream," Jessie said happily.

"Jessie, look at the counter," Benny beamed. He pointed toward the pots of chocolate, butterscotch, marshmallow, and raspberry sauces that were being heated over small burners. Festive jars of sprinkles, candy, and fresh fruit lined the rest of the counter. Over it was a sign that said: MAKE YOUR OWN BENNY SPECIAL SUNDAE.

"Oh, it looks beautiful in here," Violet said admiringly.

Mr. Brown beamed as he greeted his company. Mr. Richards had come back to see how the Shoppe was faring. Eric and his brothers and Mrs. Saunders were also among the many guests. Simone, Brian, Ruth, and Tom carried trays of fresh lemonade in sparkling glasses.

"Tom, you came back!" Benny almost shouted when he saw his favorite waiter.

"Yes. Once we found out what had been happening around here, Ruth and I decided to come back. Mr. Brown needs the help,

and we like working here better than any-where," Tom said.

"I'm glad to see so many people from the neighborhood," Grandfather observed as he helped himself to some strawberry ice cream.

"Good choice. I just made it this morn-ing," Mr. Brown said, coming by with Mr. Richards.

"Hello, James," Mr. Richards greeted his old friend. "I heard your grandchildren saved the Shoppe."

"Well, they helped," Mr. Alden answered modestly as he put his arm around Violet.

"Oh, Mr. Brown. Brian has been telling about all the problems you've had in your parlor," Mrs. Saunders called as she came toward them. She balanced her sundae in one hand and adjusted her long scarf with the other. She towered over Mr. Brown in her high spiked heels.

"Yes," Mr. Brown nodded solemnly, "but I hope all that trouble is behind us, since I had someone come in and fix the old clock."

"Oh, I'm sure it is," Mrs. Saunders said. She looked genuinely concerned. "Listen, I hope you didn't think I was trying to take some business away from you with my truck."

"I did think so at one time," Mr. Brown admitted.

Mrs. Saunders put her sundae down. "I know I've been difficult," Mrs. Saunders said. "It's just so hard to start a new business, especially when there's someone in town who carries better ice cream than I do."

Violet, Henry, and Mr. Alden looked at Mrs. Saunders in surprise.

"Oh, yes," Mrs. Saunders admitted. "I've always been a little jealous of the parlor, but I would never do anything to hurt a fellow ice cream maker. I know how hard we work," she added looking at Mr. Brown, who nodded.

"You know, I've been thinking," Mrs. Saunders continued. "Greenfield is so small. I'm going to try the bigger towns like Silver City during the week. I can come to Greenfield on weekends when we both have a lot of business."

Mr. Brown chuckled. "You shouldn't feel

you have to do that," he said. "I'm sure with the summer coming, there will be more than enough business in Greenfield for both of us."

Jessie waved to Simone and her red-haired friend. "Oh, Jessie, I'd like to introduce you to Martin," Simone said proudly. "We've just started, uh . . . going up. Is that how you say it here?"

"Going *out*," Jessie said and smiled while Martin blushed. "I'm happy to meet you," she said. "So that's what was going on," she whispered to Simone when Martin went off to get more sprinkles.

"Jessie, you didn't think Martin or I were involved in the mystery?" Simone looked surprised.

"I wasn't sure, especially after Violet saw you hiding your note." Jessie was forced to admit.

"Oh, that!" Simone said smiling. "Martin often wrote sweet little notes to me while I worked."

Before everyone sat down to eat, Mr. Brown gave a speech, but just a short one.

He didn't want everyone's ice cream to melt while he spoke.

"Thank you so much for coming," he began. "I know we've had a little trouble getting started without Mr. Richards, but those problems are behind us. From now on, we'll all make sure to have enough fresh ice cream, whipped cream, and any sauce you like on hand."

"Suddenly, everyone heard the old clock chiming. "Ding ding ding ding!"

"Look!" Benny exclaimed. "The old clock is fixed."

Everyone cheered and began eating.

GERTRUDE CHANDLER WARNER discovered when she was teaching that many readers who like an exciting story could find no books that were both easy and fun to read. She decided to try to meet this need, and her first book, *The Boxcar Children*, quickly proved she had succeeded.

Miss Warner drew on her own experiences to write the mystery. As a child she spent hours watching trains go by on the tracks opposite her family home. She often dreamed about what it would be like to set up housekeeping in a caboose or freight car — the situation the Alden children find themselves in.

When Miss Warner received requests for more adventures involving Henry, Jessie, Violet, and Benny Alden, she began additional stories. In each, she chose a special setting and introduced unusual or eccentric characters who liked the unpredictable.

While the mystery element is central to each of Miss Warner's books, she never thought of them as strictly juvenile mysteries. She liked to stress the Aldens' independence and resourcefulness and their solid New England devotion to using up and making do. The Aldens go about most of their adventures with as little adult supervision as possible — something else that delights young readers.

Miss Warner lived in Putnam, Connecticut, until her death in 1979. During her lifetime, she received hundreds of letters from girls and boys telling her how much they liked her books.